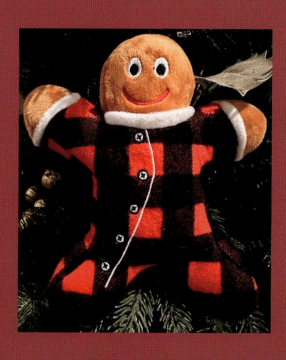

to: nigel
love: Luke
x

Dedication

To the kids of all ages who read this book series aimed toward a better humanity, because we can accomplish great things together.

To Nigel, because life has been a great adventure with you, and I have learned from you as well.

To my family, because you hold my heart, believe in me, and support and inspire me every day.

To humanity, because we have great potential.

With all my love,

Brooke C. Feeney, PhD

The Marvel of Christmas Time (Nigel's Noel)
Nigel's Neighborhood Series
Copyright © 2023 Toward A Better Humanity, LLC

All rights reserved. No part of this book may be reproduced or transmitted in any form or by any means without the written permission of the author and publisher, except in the case of brief quotations embodied in critical articles and reviews. Please refer all pertinent questions to the publisher.

Library of Congress Cataloging-in-Publication Data is available.
First Edition, 2023
Book design by Brooke Feeney with personal and family photographs
Book editing by Joyce Feeney
ISBN: 978-1-959045-02-1 (hardcover)

Printed in the USA (Signature Book Printing)

Published by Toward A Better Humanity, LLC

Visit towardabetterhumanity.com or nigelsneighborhood.com for other books in the Nigel's Neighborhood series, and for other information, products, and services aimed toward a better humanity.

ISJ

towardabetterhumanity.com
nigelsneighborhood.com

THE MARVEL OF CHRISTMAS TIME

NIGEL'S NOEL

BY BROOKE C. FEENEY

Nigel's Neighborhood Series

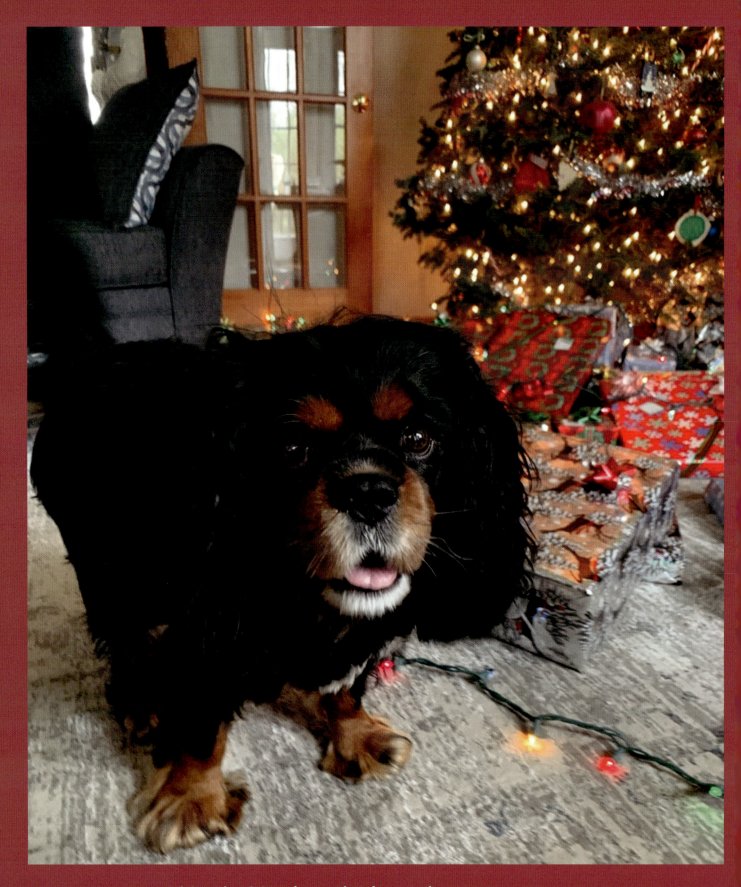

Hi. I'm Nigel. And I love Christmas time.
The biggest reason I love it is because people are better
at Christmas time than any other time of the year.
They are different in a wonderful way!

So I wrote a poem about it, like the poem "Twas The Night Before Christmas" – but different!

I call mine, The Marvel of Christmas Time.
I also call it, Nigel's Noel.

I hope people will read my poem every Christmas season and try hard to keep the spirit of Christmas all year long!

The Marvel of Christmas Time (Nigel's Noel)

Every day in December leading up to Christmas Eve,
I think about how the Christmas season makes people merry.
And about how the season makes people believe
that anything is possible for them to achieve.

People are light-hearted and happy, it seems.
They more often say hello, thank you, and please.
They better attend to each other's needs.
And they look for more ways to do good deeds.

At Christmas time people are more careful about the words they speak.
They are also more careful about the words that they tweet.
People wish joy to the world and choose to live in peace.

During Christmas time people more clearly see
what is important in life, and they are kinder with ease.
They are more patient with each other, and arguments cease.
People want to act nice instead of naughty.

At Christmas time people see that we are all on the same team.
They include others they normally wouldn't think to receive.
They don't view anyone as out of their league.
Everyone belongs; togetherness is achieved.

People take time out to gather and meet
family and friends they don't often see.

They take time to recharge, to relax, and to breathe.
They remember to play and do fun activities.

At Christmas time everyone works hard to relieve
the burdens of those who have great needs.
They make sure everyone has enough food to eat,
that everyone has a warm place to sleep,
and that everyone has warm shoes on their feet.

They make sure homeless people will not freeze,
that they are safe inside and have enough heat,
so they won't get sick and sneeze and wheeze.

At Christmas time people help those who are lonely,
and they help sad people to cope with their grief.
They work hard to help those who have a disease.
And for those who need it, they will give up their seat.

At Christmas time no one wants to be mean.
They are more careful about how they let off steam.
Even bullies are often brought to their knees.
People stop all the screams and the schemes and come clean.
They ask for forgiveness and work to redeem.

People make promises they more frequently keep.
They are careful to be truthful and not to deceive.
They become their true selves and live genuinely.
And that helps them to have higher self-esteem.

People who have been harmed are more willing to release
feelings of resentment, bitterness, and negativity.
So they have fewer headaches to try to relieve.
And they no longer feel like they are paddling upstream.
They can better concentrate on achieving their dreams.

Even strangers are friendly and take time to greet.
They bake for each other and share special treats.
People remember their morals, traditions, and beliefs.
They are quicker to notice when there is a need.

People send cards to each other and go on shopping sprees
to buy gifts for others; there is no greed.
At Christmas time people look for others to feed.
People visit each other and don't want to leave.

As Christmas approaches people count down the weeks.
They light up their homes and their hometown streets.
They create the most beautiful, amazing scenes
that have very happy and meaningful themes.

At Christmas time people hang a wreath that has pinecones, berries, and holly leaves. They bring out their special holiday antiques. A lot of decorations are red and green.

People hang stockings on mantles, some with names that are weaved.
And together they decorate Christmas trees
with candy canes and ornaments that have special memories.
There is talk about elves who make toys and keep track of all deeds.

At Christmas time everyone has glowing cheeks
when they go out in the cold to sing carols in the streets,
or to see the neighborhood lights and the uplifting scenes,
or to visit a display of a nativity.

People have fun together under the winter moonbeams.
They sled and build snow-people in the snow and the sleet.
On cold winter nights everyone wears coats and long sleeves.
Then at home they keep warm by the fire in their fleece.

At Christmas time kids go to bed easy and don't make a peep.
They try hard to keep their rooms very tidy and neat.
They eat all their veggies, even their peas.

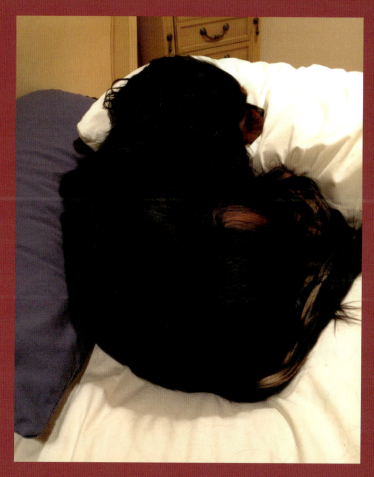

Siblings are kind to each other and don't often tease.
They stop treating each other like pesky fleas.
Together they build their happiest memories.
These are kids of all ages –
   including grandparents and teens!

Christmas time is very special for all the kiddies
who track Santa's progress on the computer screen
because traveling far in one night requires great speed.
They listen for sleigh bells and hope to see
Santa making an appearance coming down the chimney.
They know they aren't supposed to peek
but hope to get a glimpse as he makes a delivery.

Kids get so excited they feel every heartbeat.
They get excited to think that Santa will sneak
into their homes to leave them some treats.
They also leave him and his reindeer some good things to eat.

Kids tiptoe and creep to have a quick peek.
But while waiting for Santa, they soon fall asleep.

They get in their cozy beds, under the blankets and sheets.
They know he won't come 'til they're having sweet dreams.

I hope every kid gets a present of my book series to read
and a cuddly Nigel plush toy they can hug and squeeze.
There's so much kids can learn and do if they only believe
and know Christmas is about more than the toys they receive
and more than Santa Claus, who seems so supreme.

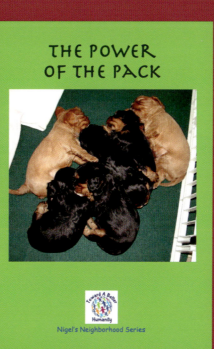
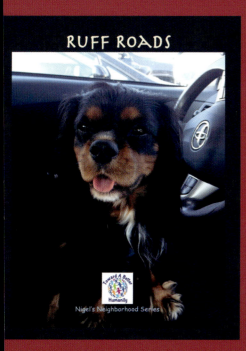

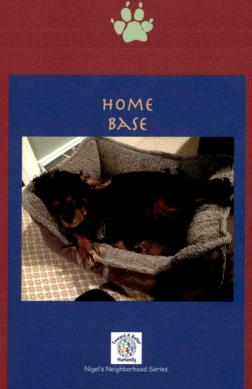

At Christmas time people cook the most amazing cuisines.
And they enjoy some special holiday sweets,
like pumpkin pie and apple pie with fluffy whipped cream.
They also have stockings that are filled with favorite candies,
like Hersey kisses, M&Ms, Snickers, and Reeses.

At Christmas time there's mistletoe that people stand underneath
to connect with each other and with kisses they greet.
They cuddle together in cozy love seats
and play happy holiday songs on repeat.
People gather for big and fun holiday feasts
and wear fun sweaters to Christmas parties.

♪ ♪
♪ J ♪
♪ I
N
G
L ♪
E
♪
B
E
♪ L
L
S ♪
♪ ♪

At Christmas time people decorate their homes with figurines,
like snow babies, angels, and Christmas villages that gleam.
When they play holiday music, everyone sings.
They sing of jingle bells and sleigh rides and beautiful things.

They build gingerbread houses made of candy.
And gingerbread cookies are a favorite cuisine.
During this season, only happy memories are retrieved.
There is "no place like home," and everyone is jolly.

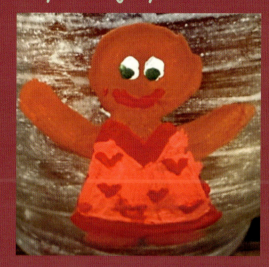

At Christmas time there are many uplifting stories on TV,
about Rudolph and Frosty and the Little Drummer Boy.
There is also a whole season of Christmas movies –
movies about miracles that help everyone believe
that they can do amazing things on their own life journeys.

At Christmas time people listen more before they speak.
They respect other people's views and respect their boundaries.
They think about what it's like to have another person's worries.
They take the time to understand instead of being in a hurry.

At Christmas time people let go of grudges that are obsolete.
They are much more willing to forgive and delete
past things that have hurt them and caused them great grief.
They smile more and show their friendly teeth.
They also let go of all their usual worries.

At Christmas time people stop trying to compete.
They no longer want to defeat or mistreat.
They instead work together to accomplish big feats.
They are open and friendly and do not critique.

When people have a light heart, they can better complete
things they couldn't do before from which they had to retreat.
They have much more energy that does not deplete.
And they find new paths on which to proceed and succeed.

At Christmas time people are generous and don't cheat.
Even the Grinch grew a big heart and stopped being a thief.
Each time people are kind, they plant a great seed
that will spread far and wide and reach the highest peaks.

At Christmas time no one wants to act like a fiend.
And when people help others, they are very discreet.
They don't need the credit for doing good deeds.
And everyone is more willing to give grace and mercy.

At Christmas time people give big tips and gratuities.
Stores give discounts to shoppers and don't charge big fees.
People work harder to promote equity
so that everyone has a home and enough food and money.
People volunteer and donate to charities.
There is a true sense of community.

☆ At Christmas time people think about their spirituality
as they celebrate the birth of a special baby.
And although people have different religious beliefs,
they remember that they're all part of one huge story
and connected to more than just what they can see. ☆

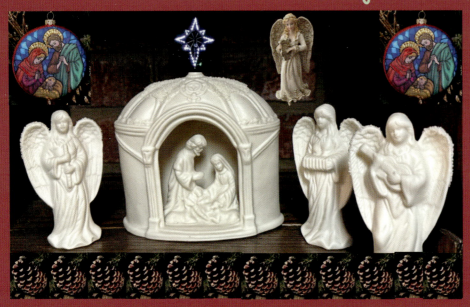

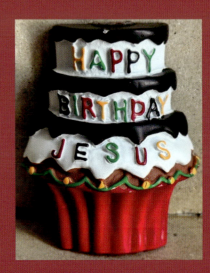

People also understand they shouldn't try to delete
anyone else's spirituality.

JOY
HOPE
LOVE
PEACE

And they remember that life is about more than trying to appease
their own lust or that of others, which will never help them to increase
the things that truly matter, like love, joy, hope, and peace.
They see that life is much bigger than a selfish focus on "me."

At Christmas time I like to sit in my window seats
and watch all the happy people and the snow flurries.
I watch the hustle and bustle in the streets and the cool breeze.
And I think about everything this special season means.

At Christmas time people remember there is a unity
that we all have with each other; no one is more elite.
No one is on top, and no one is beneath.
All humans are the same; they are all human beings.

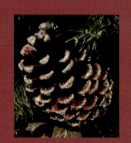

In fact, every one of us are the same species and breed.
We all want to be loved and accepted. We all need to eat and sleep.
We all need air to breathe, and we all the same way bleed.
We all can feel joy and pain, and we all have the same basic needs.

We all want to pursue our dreams. We all want to be safe and free.
We all are better together; we've been connected throughout history.
We should always help each other because we are all on the same team.

At Christmas time people remember this creed.
At Christmas time everyone truly beams.
At Christmas time everyone is very upbeat.
At Christmas time the greatest love is unleashed.
It is only kindness and cheer that is purposefully leaked.
Everyone's light gets brighter and does not decrease.
This kind of behavior is in everyone's genes.
That's why it is always so hard to conceive
why this doesn't happen every day of every week.

That's why people get sad when the season leaves.
That's why Christmas time can be so bittersweet.
That's why people want to start celebrating early.

But why is it only at Christmas time that people believe
that everyone in the world can live in peace?
That isn't the way it has to be.
Kindness should not be temporary and brief.
And good behaviors should not be a rarity.

It is truly one of my biggest pet peeves
that the whole world doesn't already live in peace.
The whole world can be one big happy family.
To understand this doesn't require a degree.

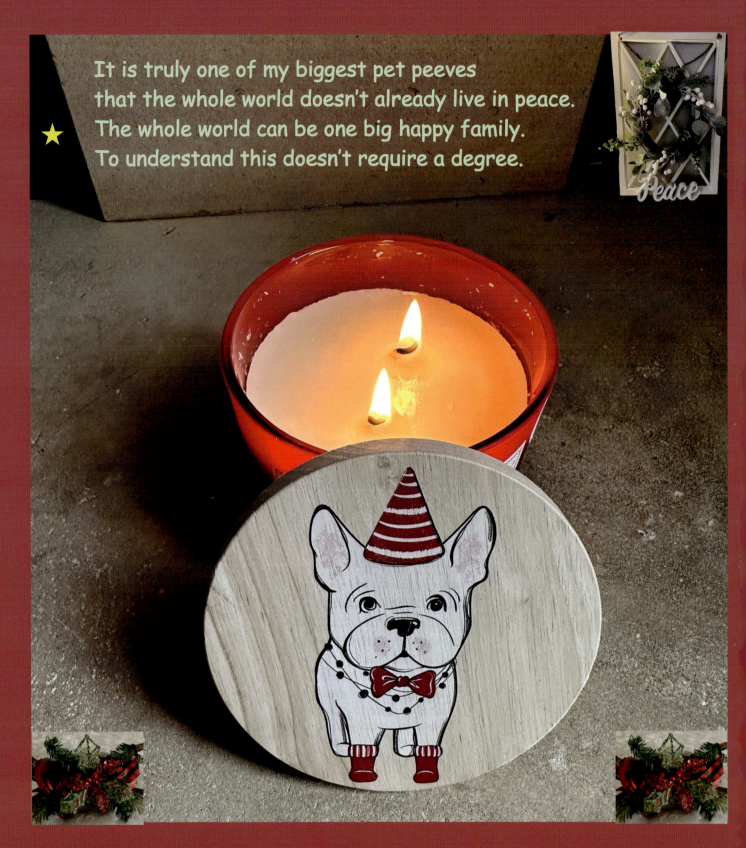

Dogs like me already have that kind of purity.
We already have that special kind of belief,
that everyone on earth is a celebrity,
that everyone, everywhere can live in peace,
and that our most beautiful life memories
are of the people we help and of those on whom we lean.

So, my most important life discovery
is that regardless of your background and personality,
everyone can be kind and respond sensitively.
And everyone can help others with their necessities.

Everyone can respect each other and accomplish great things.
Everyone in the world can choose peace and security.
Everyone in the world can become who they were meant to be.
And everyone in the world can live in victory.

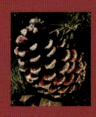

So, at Christmas time I will make this concrete.
It doesn't matter if you are large or medium-sized or petite.
It doesn't matter your color or your nationality,
or if you are small and hairy and multi-colored like me.

Every single one of us can take the lead
to make sure that all year long, these important things we seek:
- the spirit of being lighthearted and kind and happy.
- the spirit of giving and looking out for those in need.
- the spirit of joining together and living in peace.

If we do this all year long, everyone will be free.
We all will be shining stars, not just in our dreams.

So, I hope this holiday you will see
that we all have great connections and stories to weave,
and that keeping the Christmas spirit all year long will be the key
to living in peace and harmony.
This can happen in every state and in every country.

With the Christmas spirit all year long, we would have a better humanity.
There would be no better time in the world than times like these.
So, my biggest Christmas wish is for a noel that will never cease. ♥

I love to learn new things. I call them Nigel's Nuggets of Knowledge. I collect these nuggets and write them in my Knowledge Notebook. Here are my nuggets of knowledge about the Christmas season:

Nigel's Nuggets of Knowledge

1. People are most lighthearted and kind and happy at Christmas time, but they can be that way all year long. If they choose to do that, we will have a better humanity and a better world.

2. People give and help others more at Christmas time than any other time of the year. They can choose to do that all year long. If they do, we will have a better humanity and a better world.

3. At Christmas time, people join together and want to live in peace. They see that we all have the same needs, we all belong, and we all are better together. If people choose to live this way all year long, we will have a better humanity and a better world.

4. People are happier during the holidays, and all the time, when they focus on important things like family and spirituality and helping others – more than on material things like receiving gifts.

Thank you for reading my Christmas poem!

I hope you will read more of my books
to discover more of my nuggets of knowledge.

Love, Nigel

About the Author

The author is Nigel's mom, who helps Nigel share his experiences and adventures in this book series. She created the company, Toward A Better Humanity (towardabetterhumanity.com), because she has a great passion for doing her part to make the world a better place. She is a social psychologist and relationship scientist (with a PhD in these fields). She has been a researcher and professor of psychology for many years, and she applies this work in creative ways toward a better humanity. The nuggets of knowledge in this book series are based on research findings that are shared with the goal of creating new generations of better humans.

Visit towardabetterhumanity.com or nigelsneighborhood.com to find other books in the Nigel's Neighborhood Series including these:

Nigel's Neighborhood

Ruff Roads

Home Base

Thankful Thoughts

Birthday Blessings

Halloween Hopes

Hairy Happenings

Nighttime Magic

The Power of the Pack

Beach Bliss

The Fountain of Pooch

And more!

Nigel's Neighborhood Series
towardabetterhumanity.com
nigelsneighborhood.com